A Day in a Colonial Home

Della R. Prescott

Alpha Editions

This edition published in 2021

ISBN : 9789354593376

Design and Setting By
Alpha Editions
www.alphaedis.com
Email - info@alphaedis.com

As per information held with us this book is in Public Domain.
This book is a reproduction of an important historical work. Alpha Editions uses the best technology to reproduce historical work in the same manner it was first published to preserve its original nature. Any marks or number seen are left intentionally to preserve its true form.

PREFACE

The average home to-day has conveniences to meet the demands of comfortable living. The heating and lighting are good. In nearly every home may be found a living room where the family assembles for rest and recreation. Here they read, sew, chat, and discuss the news. Similar scenes occurred in the colonial days, but in quite a different room. The kitchen took the place of our modern living room. The life of the colonists centered in it, for in the kitchen was the fireplace, often the one source of heat in the whole house. Its warmth and cheer and its use as a place for cooking made it the heart of the home. Here it was that the family interests and activities were centered; all the family group collected here to share the joys and sorrows of life.

HOW THE STORY CAME TO BE WRITTEN

A Father came into the Newark Museum to ask help of the educational adviser.

"I cannot get my children interested in their ancestors," said he. "They don't feel any pride in being descended from a lady who came over in the Mayflower. They say, 'Oh, Charlie's uncle came over in a private yacht, and Mike's brother is going over in an aeroplane.' What shall I do? If we were living at the old homestead, I could show them the hole in the shutter through which the Indian shot their great-uncle, and the oven by the fireside where their great-grandmother cooked for the continental soldiers, and the wedding dress of their grandmother. But the old place was sold, and everything is scattered."

"Bring your children to the Museum," said the educational adviser. "We will show them colonial costumes and candle-molds and Indian arrows."

"I'll try it," said the father, "but it won't be the same."

Then came a teacher.

"I wish," said she, "that I could make history alive to my pupils. They don't care how many men were killed in the battle of Monmouth, or what the date was when Washington crossed the Delaware."

"We will send you some dolls in colonial costume and an old wool-carder," said the educational adviser.

"Thank you," said the teacher. "Of course, those things will be better than nothing."

It was this need to see "the real things" that caused the Museum to build in its big hall at the top of the Newark Library a colonial kitchen, and fill it with colonial furnishings. Then the students from the Normal School dressed up in colonial clothes and went to work in the kitchen, spinning, making candles, and sewing carpet rags, and explaining these things to the children who flocked in to visit them.

Next Miss Prescott began to play with the children who flocked there, and then the Andrews children of this story were born.

The six or eight thousand children who were taken by their teachers to see this kitchen during the ten weeks that it stood there, many of whom then took their parents to see it, will perhaps read this story about the labors, and the play, and the love-making of Mary Jane, with interest.

Any group of manual training boys and domestic art girls can put up such a kitchen, dress the characters, and act out such a story, and in many American neighborhoods they can borrow "real things," for their stage properties.

Of course, the story was not written to stimulate handwork or theatricals. Nor was it written to Americanize, or re-Americanize anybody. But simple stories without ingenuity of plot or striking incident have always been told by parents and grandparents and maiden aunts to the delight of children. "Tell us what happened when Grandpa was a miller"; "Tell us about when you went to school through the woods"; "Tell us how the bear frightened Great-Aunt." These are the demands of children of all nations. The peculiarity of our situation is that so many of our children are step-children, half-children, adopted children. It is a mercy that there is an inheritance not only of blood, but of memories, of ideas, and of hopes.

If this story stimulates emulation of the real virtues of our forefathers, who founded the country, and hence leads to real patriotism, it will have achieved the desire in the hearts of the authors and publishers.

A Day in a Colonial Home

Mary Jane awoke, startled. Had she overslept and not heeded her father's call? She jumped out of bed on to the strip of rag carpet laid on the cold floor. The chill of the early May morning made her shiver, and, with motherly care, she turned and straightened the patchwork quilt on her two sisters, mischievous Abigail and gentle little Dorothy, who were sleeping warmly in their feather bed. The world was a-quiver with life and sound. Mary Jane looked anxiously through the small-paned window. Surely, Providence would grant a pleasant day for the last of the housecleaning! Her mother was ill with the new baby brother and the kitchen must be cleaned before she was about again. It was not easy to do the work as well as her mother would have done it, but a bright, sunshiny day would help.

The sun was just rising and a cool, northwest breeze was blowing the mist from the pond and gully. The sunlight sparkled on the pond which lay across the foot of the field and the breeze blew it into dark blue ripples. Mary Jane dreamed a minute. John Lewis must be in port, she thought, and perhaps he would be home to-day. His father's whaler, the *Breezy Belle*, had reached Gloucester the first of the week. If she planned well and hurried the work she might be able to go down to Jenny Lewis's in the afternoon to see her new dresses. Jenny Lewis was John's sister, and she had more pretty clothes than any girl in town. It would be a welcome change to visit her before supper. The past week of housecleaning had been a busy one, for the girls had cleaned the dooryard and the entry as well as the back room and the loft bedroom. Their mother, before her illness, had cleaned and aired her best front room and put back in their places the few pieces of furniture which stood in this cold and little-used room.

The well-sweep creaked in the breeze, and a whiff of the smoke of the kitchen fire, pouring out of the chimney, blew up the stairway. Mary Jane straightened her simple gray dress, folding a fresh white kerchief across her breast. The neighbors called her smart and comely. She was sixteen, and tall and strong, the oldest of eight children. Her brothers and sisters knew her to be gentle as well as firm and just. They never shirked Mary Jane's orders, but they carried to her their bruised toes and cut fingers, the stitches dropped in their knitting, the knots tied in their patchwork. She bound up their hurts and set them to work again.

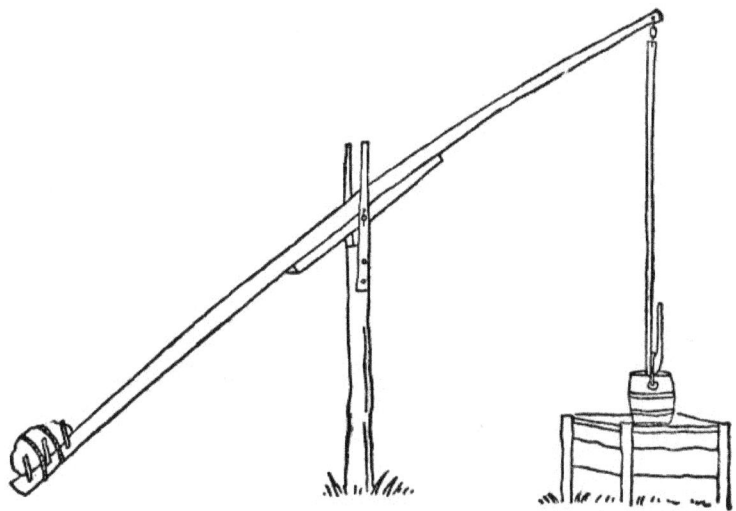

FIGURE 1. WELL AND WELL-SWEEP

"Daughter," called her father from the foot of the stairs, "the day comes on apace, and it promises a clear sky for your cleaning. Grandmother is tending your mother and the new babe, but John and I will need the porridge hot when we come back from foddering."

Mary Jane answered her father gravely and picked up the candle to take with her to the kitchen. She called the older of her sisters. The three all slept in the low-ceilinged upstairs chamber. "Come Abigail! You are in truth a sleepyhead. Come! Everything's awake, and we have much to do! Father has called and indeed you must hurry."

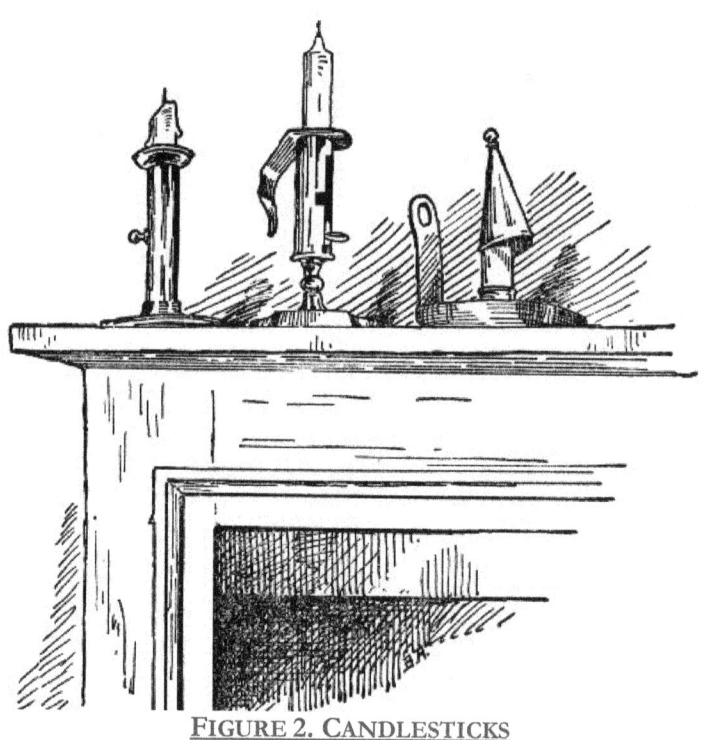

FIGURE 2. CANDLESTICKS

In the kitchen a glowing bed of red-hot coals burned on the hearth, streaks of sunlight glanced through the eastern windows and touched the snowy, coarse cloth on the large dinner-table. Soft reflections shone from the pewter porringers hanging on the dresser; a sunbeam flecked with bright light the brass candlestick which Mary Jane set near its mate on the mantel over the hearth. In the south windows red geraniums blossomed and there was an atmosphere of homely cheer and comfort in the room. All winter, the family had gathered in the kitchen and, in its warm cosiness, Mary Jane had spun, darned mittens and knit stockings. She loved the kitchen, and she worked there happily and energetically, putting into her tasks that same heartfelt devotion to duty that her great-grandfather had brought across the sea to the Massachusetts colony more than a hundred years before.

Her mother called quietly from the nearby bedroom, and Mary Jane tiptoed in. The baby was asleep and the sight of him in his helplessness and of her mother, always so strong and active, lying now so quiet and helpless at the beginning of a busy day, stirred her strangely. She bent awkwardly and kissed them, and blushed as she straightened up. Kisses were rare in her home, and she was surprised at herself. Her grandmother came in, and a commotion from the kitchen warned her that the boys were awake. Her three younger brothers, steady Thomas, and the twins, Asa and George, slept in the turn-down bed in the corner of the kitchen. They tumbled out and helped and punched each other into their clothes.

"No shoes and stockings to-day, boys," Mary Jane called. "Housecleaning time, and shoes have barely lasted through the frost."

Going to the table in the corner, she poured water into the wash basin. She washed her face and hands in the cold water, newly drawn from the well, gasping with the shock of its coldness, and rubbed her face briskly with the linen towel which hung over a roller on the door.

Suddenly the back entry door swung open, and roly-poly Sam Dodd came in, swinging an iron pot.

"Good-morrow, neighbors! Can you lend us a coal? As the weather grows milder I fear we tend our fire none too carefully."

"Did you know John Lewis had come home?" he called to Mary Jane. "Some of us stopped to see him last night and Jenny came out and two or three of the neighbors. Mother says it is ungodly the way Cap'n Lewis dresses Jenny. 'Fine feathers don't make fine birds,' she says, and Jenny doesn't work enough to pay the Cap'n. She's a fair gad-about. He toils mightily to get the whale oil to buy her gowns. John seems real pleased to be home, Mary Jane. He asked where you were."

Grandmother came into the kitchen as Sam started out with his borrowed fire.

"Pray tell thy mother, Sam, that the candles she helped us to make last fall are lasting well. We have treasured the choice green bayberry candles. Your mother will remember the day she helped me pick the bayberries for them. Now we do not need so much candle light, as the days grow longer. Thank her kindly for the bowl of rich soup she sent Daughter Andrews. Daughter will soon be up and about. Our new babe is six days old and strong and lusty. Hear how he cries."

FIGURE 3. PORRINGER OR SHALLOW BOWL

Sam grinned and bore off his coals fallen from the burning sticks; while Grandmother took the bowl of porridge in to her daughter.

FIGURE 4. CAST-IRON SKILLET

Drawing the settles up to the table Mary Jane placed her father's chair at one end and her mother's at the other for Grandmother. Abigail and Dorothy seized the small brothers and sisters and scrubbed them clean. Whereupon the children took their porringers and wooden bowls from the dresser and stood in their places behind the settles. Abigail strained into a pail the warm, frothy milk which John, the oldest brother, had brought in, and Dorothy filled the large pewter tankard with cool milk from the cellar way. Mary Jane bustled about. She dished up from the steaming kettle on the hearth the corn meal mush, or hasty pudding, and added a large, thin Johnny cake, which she had browned in the skillet. The children folded their hands and bowed their heads. Grandmother had returned to the table. Father leaned over the high back of his chair and asked the Heavenly Father's blessing on home and family and sought guidance in the tasks of the day.

FIGURE 5. TIN KITCHEN OR ROASTER

FIGURE 6. PLATE-WARMER

Mary Jane admired her father more than anyone else in the world. Wasn't he always right? She wondered. This morning while she sat with bowed head she asked herself, wistfully, if her father ever found it hard to decide between pleasure and duty. What would he say if he knew how much she wanted to see Jenny Lewis's new clothes? Would he think her frivolous? As she raised her eyes, she found her father looking quietly at her. Somehow, she seemed to feel as if he understood her better than she did herself and she sat up straight and proud because he was her father. She felt certain that he would choose his duty however hard he found it.

As Mary Jane ate her mush and milk, she planned her day and thought occasionally of Jenny Lewis. In Jenny's home they used a tin kitchen, or roaster, for their goose. But Mary Jane's family were poor, and they used a home-made device for roasting their goose. To a string hung in the fireplace Mary Jane would tie the goose's leg and Asa would sit in front of the fire and twist the string, so that the goose might become evenly browned. Jenny's mother used a plate-warmer, made with one side open to the heat, but Mary Jane would dip her plates into a kettle of hot water and never envy her friends their extra comforts and luxuries. However, Mary Jane *did* have a lively interest in new things and pretty clothes, and she said to herself that she would get through her work and have an hour or two before supper to visit Jenny whether or no.

Her father had set the churn near the hearth and the cream was warm enough for Thomas to beat. The brick oven was well heated, and she could bake apple pies, using the last of the dried apples. George should take down the few strings of apples which were left hanging on the kitchen rafters, and Dorothy should wash them at the well. It would not take long for Dorothy to clear away the dishes and fold the table-cloth and napkins. The family had few dishes and most of these were pewter bowls and porringers. A few blue dishes of Grandmother's, that she had brought from England, were left. These were used only on rare occasions. Mary Jane would wash them herself. The silver spoons and Mother's white-handled knives must be scoured with care. Abigail should attend to them and the pewter and the tin-lined copper kettles. Abigail liked to make them shine and Mary Jane knew that when one's heart is in a task the work goes quickly. There was always wool to card, and the small boys might do this in odd moments. When the fireplace was cleaned out, one of the boys must empty all the ashes into the leach barrel. Through the winter the family had saved the ashes and all grease from cooking and butchering and, in the fall, Mother would make soft soap. Mary Jane's mother and grandmother always had good luck with their soft soap, and in the clear jelly-like substance there remained little trace of the rancid grease and strong lye from which it had been made.

The simple but nourishing breakfast was soon over. Father spoke occasionally to John about the work of the day. "The flax patch must be harrowed and sowed and the sods turned for the corn," he said.

"This is a likely drying day, John; the wind and sun will draw the dampness from the earth, and take the dust from your rugs, too,

Daughter," he added, as he rose and picked up his broad, soft hat.

"Remember, children, that your mother has taught you to work quickly and with care. Show that you have learned your lesson well. Boys, stand ready to handle the dasher, or turn the roast. Come, John."

Breakfast finished, all became bustle and stir. Grandmother slipped briskly to her large, wool spinning-wheel. She was white-haired and full of years, but still she plied her task of spinning energetically and skilfully. She had learned it long before in a shire of England where wool was raised and made into cloth. Grandmother was graceful and dignified in carriage; for many years of her life she had walked back and forth at her wheel, lightly poised and alert. She lifted her spinning-wheel, and, with awkward help from Thomas, carried it into Mother Andrew's room.

PLATE II. COLONIAL FIRESIDE

FIGURE 7. WOOL SPINNING-WHEEL

"I must needs be out of thy way, Mary Jane, and will spin in thy mother's room to-day."

But Grandmother soon returned, holding the baby in the crook of her left arm. She seated herself near the fire and unwrapped many layers of soft woolen covers from little Samuel. Dipping her elbow into the basin of warm water at her side, she found it just right and bathed the baby quickly, wrapped him again in the folds of the flannel, and retied his little cap. She then put him in the cradle, and called Thomas to rock him to sleep.

FIGURE 8. A CRADLE

Mary Jane told her brothers and sisters what she expected of each of them before she pulled out her rolling-board and started to make pie-crust.

Abigail banged the churn dasher up and down and thought eagerly of the pewter and brasses to be polished.

"Thomas, methinks the wee child must be asleep. Stretch up to this churn dasher and prove yourself a dashing knave," she said.

FIGURE 9. WOODEN CHURN

"Abigail, teach not to children such play on words," chided Mary Jane.

Abigail frowned and said, "You were not always so proper in your speech, Mary Jane, before John Lewis came a-courting."

Mary Jane, flushed and flustered, knocked her cap awry, and accidentally wiped a floury hand across her cheek.

"Do you suppose that I shall be thus improved when someone comes a-courting me?" Abigail went on. "What do you think John Lewis may have made you? He has had time enough for many a turn of the hand. It is full three months since the whaler put out from Gloucester. Do you think that even a slow-witted fellow like your John may have speed in his fingers? Perchance he whittles faster than he talks?"

"Abigail," Mary Jane interrupted, "the butter must have come. Run out to the well for fresh water. I will gather the butter while you are gone. Curb your saucy tongue, sister. Mistress Dodd is coming up the road with her pot of beans, and I would not have her hear your foolish gossip."

"John wants the flint-lock, Mary Jane. Pass it down to me quickly. Oh hurry, kindly," Abigail called as she tumbled in at the doorway. The little boys followed close at her heels. "The dog has dug out a woodchuck in the stone wall, near the flax patch, and John thinks he can pot him. Do hasten, Mary Jane! Your fingers were not always thumbs."

The gun was loaded, for when it was wanted it was wanted quickly, and loading was no quick matter. Throwing it over her shoulder as John would have done, Abigail ran from the house.

Dorothy could not bear to have killed even a woodchuck who ate the flax plants. Mary Jane knew how the child loved all dumb creatures, and she sent her out into the south door-yard, patchwork in hand. Dorothy sat down on the door-step and sewed. She was setting patchwork blocks for Mary Jane's new quilt. It was a "Job's Trouble" pattern and there were in it many hexagonal blocks of real India chintz, and French calicoes that Jenny Lewis had given Mary Jane. Dorothy sewed over and over with painstakingly small stitches. But the spring day enticed her, and she stole away from her stint. She poked with a stick among the roots and dried leaves in the garden border, and thought eagerly of the colors and sweet odors soon to awaken there: hollyhocks and purple stocks, candytuft and pinks, Sweet William, by the door-step, and love-lies-a-bleeding, Queen Margarets, larkspur, tiger lilies and bouncing-bet, and sunflowers to be planted here and there with corn. Dorothy played only a few minutes, for conscience urged her to pick up the unfinished square of patchwork, and she soon went back into the house. Mary Jane bade her show Mistress Dodd into their mother's room, for her own arms were deep in the butter-bowl.

<u>FIGURE 10. FLINT-LOCK GUN AND PISTOL</u>

After Abigail had helped dig out the woodchuck, she brought in the two pails of clear rinsing water for the butter, and hastened to start her own task of the day. The pewter and copper should be made to shine as never before. She arranged on the far end of the dinner-table, pewter porringers, solid silver spoons, the pewter tankard and one large pewter plate and several small ones, the long-handled brass warming pan, two tall brass candlesticks and the snuffers from the mantel. She even removed the flint-lock pistols from their holsters beneath the mantel. Their brass mountings were dull and lustreless. She looked longingly at the brass clasps of Father's large Bible. When Mary Jane was elsewhere it might be possible to make them shine as they should.

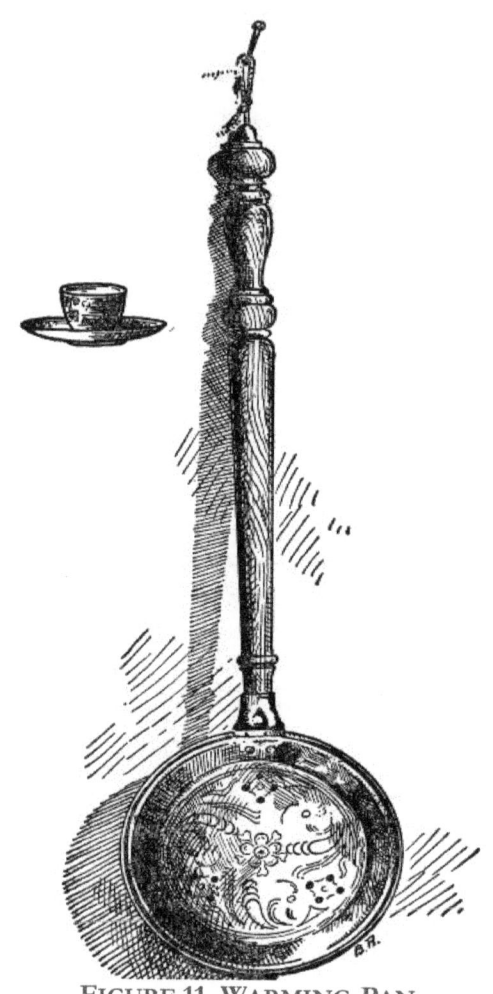

FIGURE 11. WARMING-PAN

"You have a lively way, Abigail, when your interest is taken. If we hasten, we may have the kitchen ordered by dinner-time."

"Who is this?" Abigail exclaimed.

FIGURE 12. SNUFFERS

Mary Jane looked up in consternation. Her father was bringing in two men; one was the minister and the other a stranger. She could hear them wiping their boots on the old rug on the porch. Abigail sprang helpfully forward to gather up and conceal her cleaning rags, and in doing so overturned the churn, half full of buttermilk! Mary Jane heard the crash, and saw the door open. Her father stepped right into the rushing stream of buttermilk before he saw there was an accident, and Mary Jane wondered stupidly why she had never noticed before how much the floor sloped toward the entry. The buttermilk ran over her father's shoes.

"This is a sad state of affairs, Daughter," her father said with grave reproof, "but we will go around by the other door. The minister has called to see your mother, and this good man, the indigo peddler, needs some breakfast. He has traveled far this morning. Attend to his needs and I doubt not he will show his gratitude in some way that will help you."

Mary Jane looked ruefully at the confusion, but gratefully to her father for his forbearance. Abigail had meant well, and accidents would happen. Even if it was housecleaning time, the peddler must be fed. Father believed that all hungry people should be treated kindly. "Better to feed a dozen ungracious ones," he said, "than to turn away one deserving and needy." Mary Jane directed Abigail to bring out cold porridge and salt fish and milk for the peddler, while she mopped up the floor.

As Mistress Dodd finished her call and came out of their mother's room, Mary Jane looked up from the floor and asked her if she would not take home a pat of new butter.

"'Twill not come amiss with hot Johnny cake, Mistress Dodd," she said, as she went on with her mopping.

"Yes, indeed, I will be glad to have it, Mary Jane, and thank you, too. What a bother to lose the good buttermilk," she added, looking at the floor. Then she slyly pinched Mary Jane's white arm.

"John Lewis came home last night, and they say he looks fine and hearty, Mary Jane. Think you he has learned to talk and ask questions? Have you an answer ready for him? Do not turn away your head, child, I mean naught by these bantering words. Later, I will send Sam for our baked beans. Thank you for letting us use your oven. Good-day, all."

Mary Jane finished cleaning up the floor and scattered the children who had gathered in the kitchen. Strangers were an event, and the young ones looked at the peddler eagerly and intently. The old man sat down and drew toward him the bowl of porridge, first taking a long draught of the buttermilk near at hand. Looking up from her task, Mary Jane reproved Dorothy for staring.

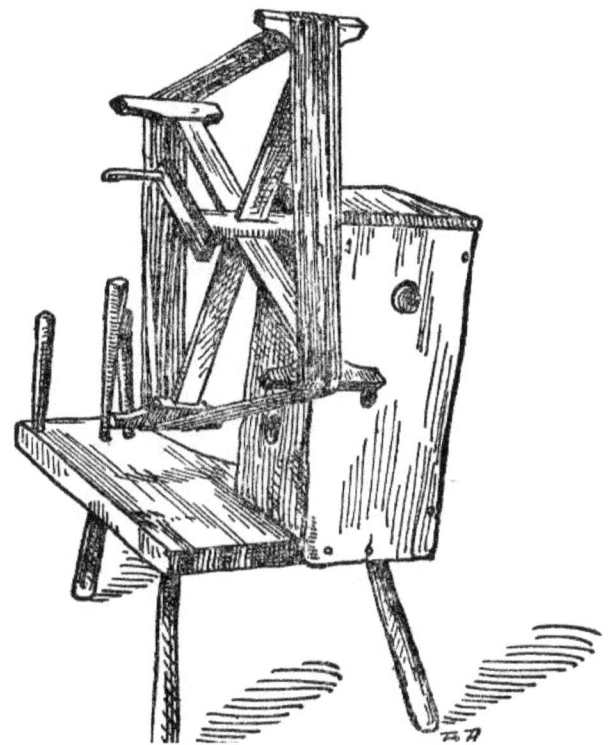
FIGURE 13. REEL FOR WINDING THREAD

"Take this flagon of buttermilk up to the flax patch. We saved this much in the churn. 'Tis ten o'clock and Father and John must be hungry. The drink will help them through the next hour."

Turning to Abigail, she suggested that she put out of doors the rocking-chair and small table. The Bible and work-basket and mother's reel might go into mother's room. Perhaps the peddler would help her move the settles out on the grass. Mary Jane herself knelt down on the hearth to take up the ashes.

The peddler jumped up. "Willing hands make light work, Mistress Mary, and out go the tables and the chairs. Back again! and now, my dears, we are ready for the old settles. Came from the sturdy land of England, these did."

Mary Jane frowned and settled her cap with dignity. "I like not too much talk. If we save our breath it will help in the lifting. Be careful of the door, please, I would not have the wood scarred."

"Clear the ways, my hearties," the peddler called, not seeming to be disturbed by Mary Jane's dignified words, "I'm the man for that job. Up you get, Mistress Mary, and down goes Jake, the indigo peddler. I can holystone a deck, why not brush up the ashes?"

Mary Jane looked doubtfully at her helper, but she soon admitted that he used the shovel and the turkey wing with a neat hand. Father said that it was often more generous to accept help than to give it, and so thinking, she turned to other work.

FIGURE 14. KETTLE

Directing Dorothy to take one kettle and Abigail the other, Mary Jane started them to cleaning the woodwork. There was plenty of hot water in the big pot which had been hanging on the crane, and there were soft soap and stout cloths. The girls were careful not to waste the soap, but they hunted for every speck and streak of dirt. Having answered a call from her mother, Mary Jane came back to the kitchen, bright-eyed, but demure. Mother had said that she wished Abigail to wash up the bricks in the fireplace, and Mary Jane would clean the windows. Master Jake had helped them generously, but they could finish up the rest of the work alone, their mother thought.

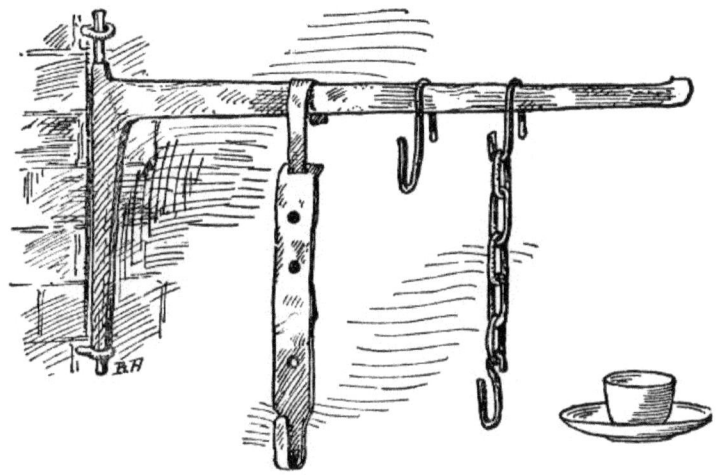

FIGURE 15. SWINGING CRANE

"Just as the Mistress says. I'll be off. Indigo has gone a-begging this morning, but perhaps I can sell some cochineal up the road. Good-day and the Lord bless ye!" So saying the old man bent to his pack and trudged away.

Abigail stood and pondered. She was mischievously interested in the change of plan. Mary Jane generally washed out the fireplace.

"What does it mean, Dorothy? Dost think John Lewis would notice if Mary Jane's hands were smutted and grimy?"

"Methinks 'tis best for us to stop talking and get to our work. Mother would have Mary Jane make a good impression. Mary

Jane is comely, and John Lewis is not a-courting *us*." Dorothy's reproof was gently made, and she smiled at Abigail.

The three sisters worked steadily and swiftly. Mary Jane appeared not to hear the whispering of the younger girls. She polished the windows, and the warm sunshine filled the room. She soon relieved Dorothy of further cleaning, and sent her into the yard under the hickory tree to sew a long seam. The child fastened her work with a sewing-bird to a little table, and sewed industriously.

John came in just then, and took down the shoemaker's last. He wanted to get out an ugly nail from his mother's shoe. She would soon be up again. Mary Jane asked him if he would take the children out to hunt for hens' nests after he had finished. She hoped to have a custard for supper.

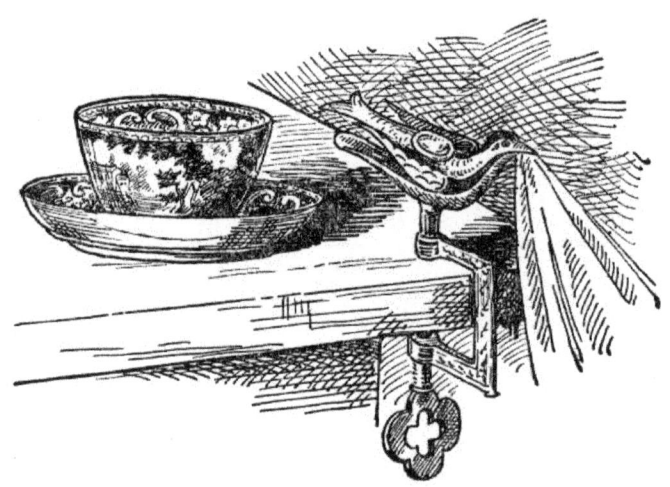

FIGURE 16. SEWING-BIRD

A little later her father followed John in from the flax patch, and the family gathered for dinner, eating cold boiled salmon and the dried-apple pie which Mary Jane had hurriedly made in the morning. These, with milk and Johnny cake, soon satisfied the hungry workers and each was back at his task.

Father and John predicted a thunder-shower in the late afternoon, and Mary Jane looked anxiously at the clouds. Perhaps the shower would go round? She was not much tired, she thought, and the work, in spite of accidents, was going well. It would be too hard if she finished the kitchen in time and then had to give up her visit to Jenny because of a thunder-shower. But after dinner the work went more slowly. It seemed as if she could not get things all finished and the kitchen looking just right. She was more tired than she had realized. But her determination to get away for a little time before supper grew with her weariness. She worked desperately to put the finishing touches on the room, and, after a while, it suited her.

Abigail and Dorothy had gone out with John and the little boys to hunt for eggs, before they washed and changed their dresses. Mary Jane's mother and the little baby brother were sleeping and her grandmother's spinning-wheel made the only sound in the afternoon's stillness. The room darkened with the coming storm. The leaves of the red geraniums moved in the rising wind, and the white, sash curtains blew out into the room. Mary Jane picked a dried leaf out of the basket of freshly laundered caps and straightened the blue calico cushion in the rocking chair.

FIGURE 17. ANDIRONS OR FIRE-DOGS

She opened the door of the brick oven where Mrs. Dodd's beans and their own had been baking since morning. The beans were baked perfectly in the round, brown pots, and their fragrant, appetizing odor filled the room. Looking about, before she went upstairs, Mary Jane felt that her mother would be satisfied with the appearance of the kitchen. The brass andirons in the fireplace and the shovel and tongs glowed from Abigail's honest rubbing. The black pots and copper kettles had been cleaned inside and out and hooked on to the swinging frame. The waffle-irons and toaster hung on the side of the fireplace and the gridiron stood on its three slender legs beside the hearth.

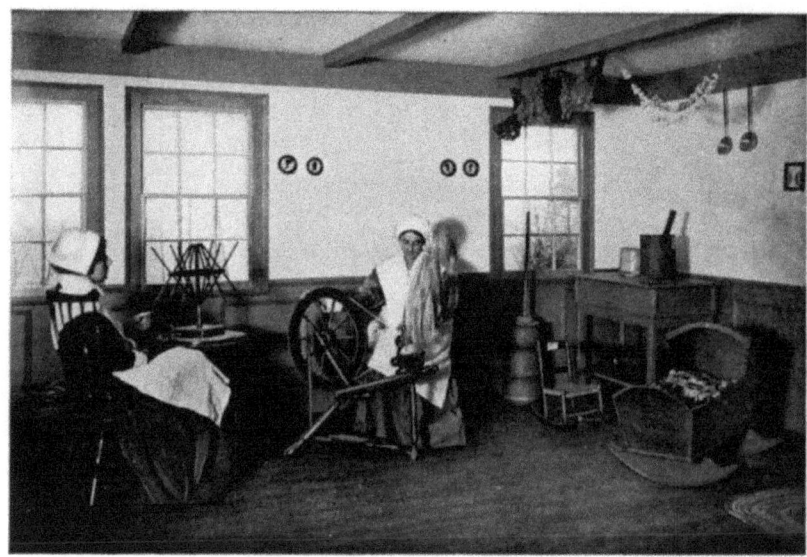

PLATE III. DOMESTIC INDUSTRY

PLATE IV. TEA TIME

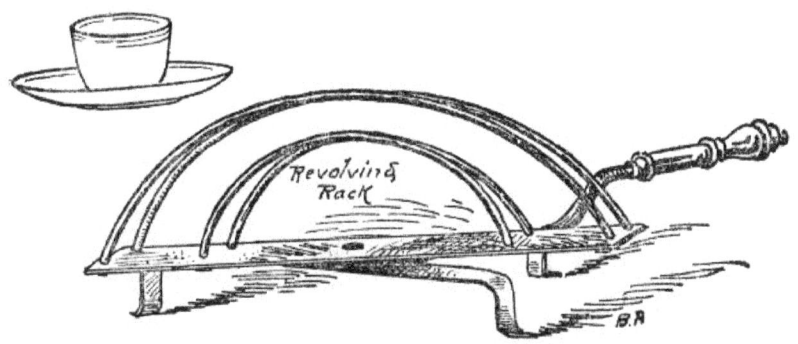

FIGURE 18. TOASTING-RACK
Revolving Rack

FIGURE 19. A GRIDIRON

FIGURE 20. KNIFE-TRAY

FIGURE 21. SPECTACLES AND BIBLE

A small fire burned red on the hearth and a gentle cloud of steam rose from the bubbling kettle. The brass warming-pan made a blob of light against the dull red bricks. The dresser was white from its recent scrubbing and the pewter on it shone brightly. Grandmother's blue plates and saucers had been rearranged on the plate rail and the spoons and white-handled knives laid back in the mahogany boxes on the dresser. John had whittled and smoothed those boxes for his mother in the winter evenings. The Bible, and the New England Primer and Father's horned spectacles lay on the small table in the corner, and the cradle, with its new pink and white checked cover, stood near the fireplace. When Mother got up, the baby would lie in that all day. The floor looked nice and clean. It had been freshly sanded and the braided rugs laid carefully in their usual places before the hearth and doorways. The old gray cat had stretched himself near the fireplace, and his friend, the dog, slept beside him.

Mary Jane noticed that the wind had blown awry Dorothy's framed sampler which hung on the wall. She straightened it and read again the words: "Honor thy father and thy mother that thy days may be long in the land which the Lord thy God giveth thee. Dorothy Ward Andrews." She read the words soberly, and thought of her own good father. Picking up her clean cap and a basin of water, she started upstairs. A sudden clap of thunder shook the house and, with the first sprinkle of rain, the kitchen door blew open and Jenny Lewis dashed in.

"Just in time, Mary Jane! I am glad you are through with your work! I have come to take you home to supper as soon as this shower blows over. John told me to tell you he would bring you home this evening. He has something pretty for you. I do not know what it is, but he made it and he feels sure that you will like it. You are too good, Mary Jane! I told John that you were kinder than I, but perhaps you would not like his homemade gift. I am very sure that I should not prefer it unless it were finer than you could buy in the shops." So talking on, Jenny pushed Mary Jane through the stairway door.

The storm drove her father out of the flax patch, and in a few minutes, he hastened into the warmth of the kitchen. His wife called from the inner room and told him that Jenny Lewis had come for Mary Jane and she hoped he would allow the girl to go down to Cap'n Lewis's for the evening. There could be no harm, the mother said, in Mary Jane having well-to-do friends. John Lewis was a sober, industrious youth, even though his sister Jenny was rather flighty. She would like to have Mary Jane go more often to visit in Jenny's home. As the mother made her ambitious little plans, the girls came into the kitchen. Mary Jane glanced shyly at her father. She was wearing her best summer dress.

"Jenny has asked me down to her house for supper, Father. The storm has passed around, and the sun is coming out. I should like to go. Everything is ready to put on the table for your supper, and Abigail can attend to the children. Jenny says she and John will walk a piece with me when I come home."

"Why, Mary Jane Andrews, I never said anything of the sort!" Jenny exclaimed, "John sent word he wanted to bring you home."

Mary Jane's father looked at her searchingly and gravely. Mary Jane had not meant to tell a fib but she was always bashful when she spoke of John Lewis. Could there be a smile in her father's eye? She thought not. She dropped her own eyes and waited. In a minute her father spoke:

"Better not go out to-night, Daughter. Your mother will be up in a day or two, and then there will be more freedom for you. Responsibility will not hurt any lass and a small disappointment is better than a pleasure taken at the wrong time."

"Tell John," her father added as he turned to Jenny, "that we shall be glad to see him when he calls up here. I hear that your father has made another successful trip. It is a hard and dangerous life he lives on the sea. May the Lord prosper him." Then Mary Jane's father went out.

Jenny flung herself into the rocker and spoke angrily to Mary Jane.

"I am glad indeed that my father is not a cross-patch! What does your father think? Just because he is one of the elders in the church must his daughter have no pleasure? He does not give you any gay dresses. Even your best dress is just this blue one with a white kerchief. It is not fair, and now he will spoil our little pleasure. I believe he likes to forbid you to do things, just because he knows you will obey. Why do you? Come with me and show your father you have a right to a few minutes in the day! Perhaps he does not approve of me! Well, I do not care. Come, Mary Jane. Come down and see my new dresses. Your father said, 'Better not go out to-night'; he did not forbid you to go. You can tell him that when you come back. Oh, what is the use of coaxing! You look just as stubborn as your father. Good-by, I am going home!"

"Come back here, Jenny Lewis!" Mary Jane called after her. "I am glad I look like my father! He has a perfect right to keep me at home if he wants to. Folks feel sorry because your father has to work so hard and spend so much of his money on clothes for you. I like pretty clothes too, but if my father thinks I am putting too much thought on myself, he tells me so. He shows me my duty."

FIGURE 22. WHEEL FOR SPINNING FLAX

Mary Jane pulled her flax-wheel toward her and whirled the wheel rapidly.

"My father believes I will grow in grace and patience for big sorrows and disappointments if I bear little ones cheerfully. What kind of practice are you getting, Jenny Lewis? It is wicked to talk about a father as you have talked about mine. I am not disappointed one bit about not going to your house. I like my homespun dresses and I can make linen as fine as you get in your dresses from England. When I get the kitchen cleaned and the floor sanded and the white curtains in place I feel happy. It is my work and it pleases my mother and I like to do it. Father does not say much about our work, because he expects us to do it well. He knows work is good for us. But what are you doing, Jenny? All you think about is pretty dresses and looking gay. I am glad Father thought I was needed here at suppertime—but I will come down to your house some other night," Mary Jane said more gently.

"Perhaps you are right, Mary Jane, but you need not get so cross about it. I may be lazy, I suppose, but I do not see what there is about work that makes you like to do it, and in disappointment, even a little one, that makes you glad to bear it."

"Jenny, I cannot explain. I like to cook and clean and spin and knit. That's the way I feel. It isn't hard. I don't mean to be conceited or think myself better than other people, but somehow when my father is strictest with me something inside of me likes it. Here comes Dorothy with a bunch of pink and white arbutus. It grows late up in the woods. How pretty it is! Our Pilgrim grandmothers must have been glad to see it peeping up from the snow after their long, hard winters. Who is this coming in with the boys? Why, it is your brother John! Jenny, will you and John stay to supper with us?" Mary Jane turned to her friend eagerly.

"Yes, Mary Jane, and I will help you with the dishes and, after supper, John shall tell us stories about his voyage. It is just as well we were disappointed! I will try to be a more dutiful daughter, Mary Jane. I guess Father and Mother like to have me visit you. They chide me for my heedless ways."

The girls and boys came trooping in together and Mary Jane pushed aside her flax-wheel and stirred the embers on the hearth, laying on fresh sticks. John Lewis met her with awkward shyness and dropping a bulky package on the chair beside her said, "Open it later, Mary Jane. It is for you. I whittled it out in spare minutes aboard the *Breezy Belle*."

Jenny called across the room.

"Hurry up, John Lewis, and all of you boys wash while we help Mary Jane dish up the beans. It is supper time, and she has asked you and me to stay. Here is Sam Dodd, Mary Jane."

"Oh yes, he wants his mother's beans. They are the ones in the back of the oven, Jenny. Please help him."

"We shall be glad to help you while your oven is being repaired, Sam. Tell your mother to send in anything she wants to have baked.

"Do open the door for him, John. It would be a pity for him to drop the beans and spoil his mother's supper."

So, laughing and hurrying, Mary Jane and her helpers soon had on the table their supper of baked beans and brown bread, custards and cool drinks of milk. After supper, Father asked his family and the company to gather for prayers at once for he had an errand up the road and wished to get back early. The planting and housecleaning days were hard ones and he knew that his folks needed to get to bed in good season if they wanted to do good work the following day.

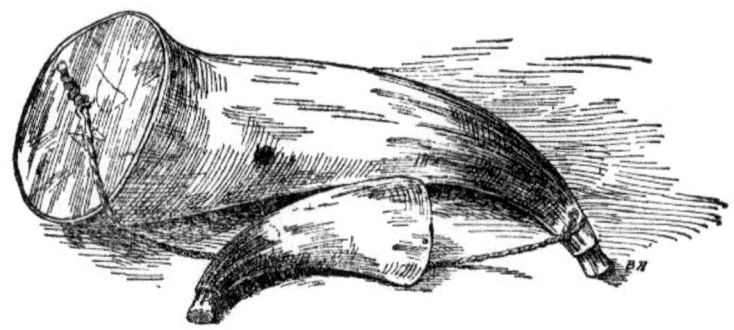

FIGURE 23. POWDER-HORN

Mary Jane placed a candle on the table near the Bible and the children drew up their stools and Father's chair. Father read the twenty-third psalm and knelt to pray. He thanked the Lord for the blessings of the day, the fair weather and plentiful food and his helpful sons and daughters. He prayed that all young souls, untried in the furnace of life, should lean on the Lord and strive to do their duty nobly as He would show it to them. He prayed earnestly and rose from his knees weary but heartened. The young folks went gravely about the task of clearing away the dishes. But when Father Andrews departed, their solemnity gave place to mirth and jolly fun. John raked open the coals and brought out a little popcorn that had lasted through the winter. Thomas agreed to pop it for them, and John took down his powder-horn. He wanted to finish whittling the design on it. Dorothy coaxed Jenny down on the settle to tell about her visit in Boston and Mary Jane brought out a skein of soft, white wool.

"Perhaps you will hold this for me, John Lewis? I am going to knit a hood for the new babe Samuel, but the wool must first be wound in a ball."

"No, Mary Jane, there is a better way to hold that worsted than on a man's outstretched arms. Open the package I brought you and look within."

Mary Jane untied the hempen cord fastened about the bundle John had brought in and the boys and girls gathered near, with jest and laughing glances. So John Lewis had made their sister something! Well, he always looked as if he liked her, but this was proof indeed. What could it be, so bulky and strange looking? Would Mary Jane never get it out? She handled the string slowly (almost lovingly, John Lewis hoped). But at last the covers fell off on her lap, and she held out a dainty and beautifully polished swift. John took it from her, and, placing it on the table, dropped over the outspread spokes, her skein of white worsted. He quickly found the end of the skein, and placing it gently in Mary Jane's hand, bade her wind the ball. As the reel turned slowly and Mary Jane's ball grew large and soft, she lifted her eyes gratefully to John Lewis. The others had withdrawn to the settles and fireplace and John made bold to whisper as he leaned across the corner of the table:

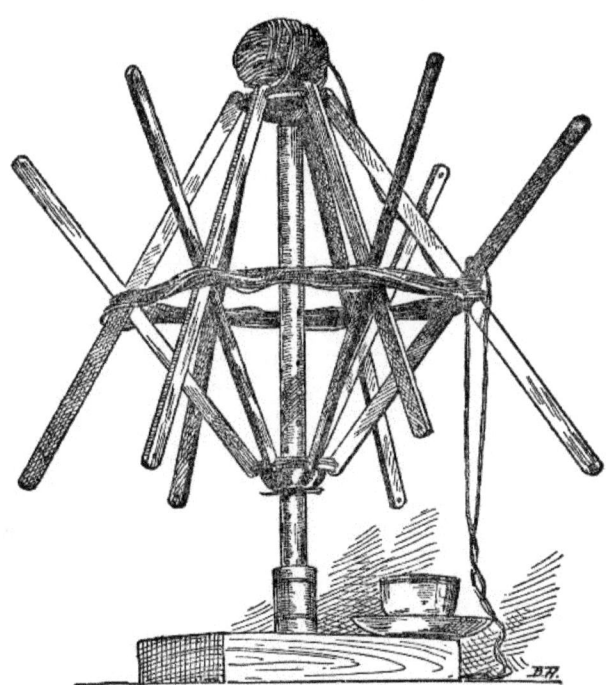

FIGURE 24. SWIFT FOR WINDING YARN

"Mary Jane, will you walk out with me on the Sabbath? 'Twill be a long six months before we put to sea again, and, perhaps, in that time you may come to like a slow fellow like me. Maybe I can make you a chest to put your caps and linens in while I am home. That would make you think of me when you put things in it after I am gone. Will you walk with me, Mary Jane?"

Mary Jane twirled the reel and examined the cunningly wrought initials of her name on the side and flushed a lovely color when she discovered J. L.—John Lewis—just below them. She gazed laughingly at John and nodded her head, but her shy whisper left him speechless:

"I do not think you are a slow fellow, John, and I like you now. I have liked you a long time! I have a chest and it is half full of fine linen. I have been busy."

"Mary Jane, did you think of me as you spun the linen and dyed the wool?"

Mary Jane nodded again and picked up her knitting-needles. Her father came in and John jumped to his feet.

"Elder Andrews, may I have Mary Jane for my wife? She likes me, she says, and we need not wait? Will you let us have the banns published this Sabbath approaching? I am twenty, sir, and Mary Jane is sixteen. That is only a year younger than my father and mother were when they married and came to the colony."

"Daughter, is this your wish?" her father asked.

A solemn hush fell on the group in the kitchen. Grandmother stood in the doorway and gazed affectionately on the oldest daughter of their family. She knew the sterling worth of the girl John Lewis desired for his wife, and she knew that if these young people married, another home would be established in the colony which would be a power for righteousness and godly living.

Mary Jane looked steadfastly at her father, and tucked her hand under John's arm as she answered:

"Yes, Father."

"Then God bless you both, my children, and may you believe all that is required in this world is for you to live justly, to love mercy and to walk humbly with your God."

So saying, he walked quietly from the room. The brothers and sisters crowded about Mary Jane and John, and Jenny whispered as she put on her bonnet: "Mary Jane, I like your father."

Mary Jane smiled gently. A peace and happiness had come into her heart that knew no words. She turned to John to say goodnight. Her father's blessing shone from her loyal, brave eyes, and John Lewis knew that he was truly fortunate among men.

HOW TO BUILD A COLONIAL KITCHEN IN SCHOOL, LIBRARY OR MUSEUM

Give to an intelligent carpenter the following directions:

Make the kitchen, if possible, as large as 16' × 20'. Put the fireplace in the center of one of the longer sides. On the opposite side make the wall the height of an ordinary table, 31", except for a space of 3' at each end, thus leaving an opening on that side about 14 feet long. Through this opening the kitchen will be chiefly viewed. At the right of the opening put a door, cut in half in the old Dutch fashion. (Plate I.)

Build the walls of "compo-board," a trade article easily obtained, and costing (January, 1921) about 8 cents per square foot. We have found nothing so serviceable as this for light and temporary interior construction. Make the walls not over 8' high. Construct rafters of thin boards—they may even be of compo-board and hollow, and lay them across from wall to wall. (Plate II.)

At one end put 2 or 3 windows. These windows should be small and have small panes. The sash need not be movable. The windows in the picture were found at a junk shop, as were also the door already mentioned and the one for the corner cupboard. (Plate III.)

Plate II shows the character of the fireplace and its size, and gives the mantel-piece in ample detail. The bricks are, of course, only such in appearance, being painted on. The crane may be a genuine old one, or of wood. The fire is made by an electric lamp, hidden in the sticks and covered with red tissue.

The wainscoting and the mantel-piece are simple in the extreme. The appearance of paneling is produced by tacking molding on the walls of compo-board, all as indicated. The ceiling is made of cotton cloth stretched tightly above the beams.

In one corner is a cupboard. This can be made, as in the picture, with an ordinary small door, or can be a genuine antique. On the walls may be hung a hood, tippets, mittens and a few other domestic articles, all as indicated. Above are peppers, a few strings of dried apples, etc. But be chary of objects and keep the whole atmosphere simple. (Plate IV.)

Paint rafters, wainscoting and cornice all the same color, as suits the taste of the constructor. The walls above the wainscoting should be very near white for lighting purposes.

Outside so place bushes like barberries that they may be seen through the windows. ([Plate III.](#))

We found it desirable to have the kitchen lighted from one end. Thus lighted it looked much like a genuine interior at sunset. To get this illumination through the windows at one end, we first reduced the general lighting of the room in which the kitchen was erected. We then placed, a few feet from the windows, a large screen of cotton cloth on which were sketched in strong color a tree against a brilliant yellow sunset sky. Right under the windows we placed several strong electric lights with reflectors, throwing a brilliant light upon the screen above mentioned. From the screen, as if from a sunset, there came a yellow light into the room, adding greatly to the beauty and attractiveness of the whole interior.

The furnishings of the room will depend on what may be found available for the purpose.

APPENDIX

FIGURE 1

Well and well-sweep. Water was rarely piped into houses and barns. Lacking a brook or spring a well was dug near the house. Pumps were expensive and not often used, but a device like this for lifting water from a well could easily be made. The pole, or sweep, was so weighted at the large end that it would almost lift the vertical stick and the bucket at the other end when the latter was full of water. A moderate pull on the vertical pole carried the bucket down to the water. When the bucket had filled a moderate lift on the pole brought it to the top. A chain from A to B gave room to lift the bucket over the curb.

FIGURE 2

Candlesticks were often of brass, though the poorer people used those made of wood, iron or tin; and three nails driven into a bit of board could serve very well. Those of brass were often beautiful.

The knob on the upright of the stick at the left slid up and down in a slot and carried with it a movable base; with this device the candle was lifted out of the upright as it burned, until the base came to the top and the last atom of the candle burned.

The central stick shows a like device, and has also a thin projecting arm of brass which could be put into a socket in the wall.

The third one has its candle covered by an extinguisher, a hollow cone, dropped on a lighted candle to put it out. The upstanding extension of brass has a hole in its end, and by this can be hung over a nail in the wall.

FIGURE 3

A porringer or shallow bowl, often of pewter and sometimes of silver, with a handle which was commonly decorated with perforations. The perforations helped to keep the handle cool. The porringer was chiefly used on the table as a dish, though food was often cooked in it also. It was most often used for serving food to children.

FIGURE 4

A cast-iron skillet with legs to lift it above the coals and ashes. As all cooking vessels were used at an open fire they were all made either to hang above it like a pot or to stand before it like a tin oven, or to rest upon its coals like a three-legged skillet.

FIGURE 5

A tin kitchen or roaster. A box of tin standing on legs and with one side open. A steel spit was stuck through the meat and the meat was fastened to it by skewers, which passed through the meat and through small holes in the spit itself. All was then placed in the roaster, which was set before the fire. The spit was turned from time to time as the cooking required. Gravy was caught in the hollow below, and some of it was now and then taken up in a spoon and poured on the meat. This was "basting." The task of turning the spit by the crank on one end of it was often given to a boy. In the homes of the wealthy and in taverns the one who thus minded the roast was often called a turn-spit. By means of simple tread-mill devices a dog was often used to turn the crank, and he then became a turn-spit dog.

FIGURE 6

A plate-warmer. This was a box of tin or sheet iron on legs, with a door in one side. It stood near the fire and in it were placed dishes to be warmed, and food that was cooked and ready to eat but needed to be kept hot until the rest of the meal was prepared, or until all the family had gathered and were ready to sit down to the table. In very cold weather the kitchen sometimes could not be kept warm, no matter how big and hot the fire in the fireplace. It was then a comfort, and almost a luxury, to have hot dishes from which to eat the food which the cold room soon chilled.

FIGURE 7

A wool spinning-wheel. The spinner walked back and forth in using this wheel, and her walk was often many miles in a day's spinning. A band of stout cord goes around the big wheel and around the spindle. A strand of wool, very light and loose, is gently drawn by hand from the distaff to the end of the finished thread which is wound about the spindle. This strand is held loosely in the left hand. The right hand on one of the spokes of the large wheel gives it a smart turn. The spinner then walks away from the machine and the spindle, swiftly turned by the momentum of the large wheel, twists the loose strand of wool into a close thread. This thread is of such length and of such size and hardness of twist as the spinner decides upon, all being dependent on the force with which the big wheel is pushed, on the thickness of the loose strand of wool, and on the way in which the spinner holds it as she walks from the wheel. The finished thread is then wound on the spindle by gently reversing the large wheel, and holding the thread at the spindle. Then the same process is repeated.

FIGURE 8

A cradle. Few colonial babies had rocking cradles as luxurious as this; indeed, few had cradles at all.

FIGURE 9

A wooden churn. Its like is used to this day. In former times churning was one of the tasks that many a farmer's boy had too much of. On the lower end of the handle, which passed down through a hole in the center of the cover, was a disk of wood, perforated and fitting loosely in the tall tub. The tub was partially filled with cream and the butter was made to "come" by moving the handle up and down and thus splashing the disk up and down in the cream.

FIGURE 10

A flint-lock gun. The flint was fastened into the hammer and, as it drove down against a curved shield, it raised a shower of sparks and at the same time lifted the shield and exposed to the sparks the powder in the pan. The powder, being thus ignited, the fire followed it through the hole into the barrel and exploded the powder in the "charge" behind the bullet or shot. All flint-locks "hung fire." That is, the pulling of the trigger did not discharge the gun as quickly as it does in modern guns where the exploding cap is connected directly with the charge in the cartridge.

A flint-lock pistol. This operated just as did the flint-lock gun.

FIGURE 11

The warming-pan. In most houses the only warm place was by the kitchen fire. In winter the bedrooms were about as cold as the weather out of doors. This made the beds far from comfortable to get into on a cold night. The warming-pan was a basin of brass or copper with a hinged cover, sometimes decorated. Hot ashes and coals from the kitchen fire were put into it; it was then carried to the bed and the hot pan was pushed up and down between the sheets until the whole bed was warm.

FIGURE 12

Snuffers. Here, as in many of the other pictures in this book, a tea-cup and saucer are placed near the drawing of the object to be described. This is added to give a correct idea of the relative size of the objects represented. In each case the object to be described and the tea-cup are drawn to the same scale; and, as you know about how large a tea-cup is, you get a clear idea of the size of the object by which it stands.

Snuffers were used to snip off the end of a candle wick. As the tallow or wax melted and burned, the top of the wick, although it was burned to a mere black bit of coal, held fast to the part of the wick which still continued to draw up the melted tallow into the flame. If this black end was not now and then picked off with the snuffers, or some other instrument, or with the fingers, it dropped over and perhaps hit the top of the candle and kept it from burning bright and clear.

The snuffers are like a pair of scissors, with a box on one blade and a cover for the box on the other. When used they were handled like a pair of scissors and the black end of the wick was snipped into the box out of sight and harm. The pointed end of one blade was used to prick up the wick if it did not stand straight or was too tightly twisted. The three legs kept the snuffers, which were sooty on the under side from being stuck into the candle flame, away from the table or the tray where they were usually kept.

The candles of to-day do not often need to be snuffed, because as their wicks, which are carefully twisted, are burned free of the tallow, wax or paraffin, they bend a little in the effort to untwist. This bending thrusts the used-up end sidewise into the hot, outer flame and there it is quite burned up. In old days the wicks were not twisted much, if at all, and so, as the candle melted from them,—they stuck up into the dull, smoky, non-burning part of the flame, and stayed there until they hung over or fell off.

FIGURE 13

A reel for winding the thread into skeins, from the spindle which was taken from the spinning-wheel as soon as it was filled. By means of a cog wheel and a worm screw within the box, and a pointer on its side, the number of turns of the reel were easily counted, and that told the length of the thread wound on it. As the wheel revolved it made a loud click for each of a certain number of turns.

FIGURE 14

Kettles were usually made of iron; these had to be cast and not wrought, but, as they were usually thick and heavy, most large kettles were made of thin brass, sometimes of copper. These tarnished easily and one of the many and not very pleasant tasks of the housewife was to keep them clean and bright.

FIGURE 15

In the fireplace was hung a swinging crane of iron. Suspended from it were hooks on which pots and kettles were hung. The hooks could be moved along the crane and were of different lengths and sometimes adjustable. The crane could thus hold several kettles at once, some in the very heat of the fire and some farther away. The fireplace was the center of the home, the one source of heat, the one place for cooking and often the one source of light at night. Many pioneers and their families had to do all their reading on long winter evenings by the light of the open fire.

When a house was built and the chimney and fireplace finished, the "hanging of the crane," the final step in preparation for housekeeping, was sometimes part of a ceremony, with Bible reading, hymns and prayers, followed by feasting and rejoicing.

FIGURE 16

All sewing was done by hand. A sewing-bird was often fastened to a table by a thumbscrew. The cloth was caught in the beak as desired and this made the sewing easier.

FIGURE 17

Andirons or fire-dogs were used in every house, for all fires were of wood and in fireplaces. The poorer people were content with very simple andirons, made of wrought or cast iron and without any ornament. In these, the standards are made tall and they have as ornaments little vase-forms of brass at their tops.

Tongs and shovel were as necessary as the andirons, and like them were often of the simplest make. These have handsome brass handles.

FIGURE 18

A toasting rack. Slices of bread were placed on edge between the curved bars, and the rack was then set before the fire. The flat strip of iron to which the bars were fastened could be made to revolve on the bar below, attached to the handle so that when one side of the bread was toasted, the other side was easily turned to the fire.

FIGURE 19

A gridiron, used not only for cooking meat but also as a rest on which to set cooking utensils of any kind, raising them above the coals below. All utensils of this type stood on legs to lift them a little above the coals and ashes.

FIGURE 20

Knife-tray, used also for spoons. It was handy and took the place of a drawer. In many of the home-made tables for the kitchen there was no drawer. The tray was usually made of wood and very simple.

FIGURE 21

Spectacles and Bible. The rings at the ends of the frames gripped the head behind the ears a little and helped to hold the spectacles more securely. The rims and frames were often made of iron and were then very heavy.

A big Bible like this, with brass corners and clasps, was in many colonial homes. From it the head of the house read aloud every morning or evening. In it, on blank leaves between the Old and New Testaments, was kept the "Family Record," that is, a list of births, marriages and deaths with dates, sometimes going back for several generations.

FIGURE 22

A wheel for spinning flax. At this wheel the spinner, almost always a woman, sat to spin. The process was quite similar to that followed with a wool-wheel; but the wheel was made to revolve by a pedal like that on a sewing machine.

FIGURE 23

A powder-horn. Powder was almost always carried in a horn. The horn was usually home made and very simple. A cow's horn, which is hollow, was patiently scraped on the inside until it was smooth and as thin as the maker desired. In the larger end was fitted a bottom of wood, and in this was fastened a ring or a nail. The small end was cut off to give a hole of proper size. In the horn was cut a rim or groove. To this groove and to the ring in the bottom a stout cord was fastened, which passed over the hunter's shoulder and held the horn at a convenient place at his right side. The opening was stopped by a wooden plug, so made that it could be easily removed and held in the teeth, so that the hunter might have both hands free to pour out the powder. Often a smaller horn was carried in the pocket to hold a finer and quicker-acting powder to fill the pan for firing. Being finer, it entered the hole more easily and joined the powder of the main charge. Being quicker-acting, it helped to lessen the "hang fire" habit.

FIGURE 24

A swift, which was fastened to the edge of a table by a thumb-screw. A skein of yarn was placed on it just as it was expanded, like an umbrella, and then, the swift turning as the yarn was pulled, the yarn could be easily wound from it into a ball or on to a spool.

FIGURE 25

A spider or skillet with a bail by which it could be hung over the fire from the crane. It also has legs for standing among the coals.

FIGURE 25. SPIDER OR SKILLET WITH BAIL

FIGURE 26. A COLONIAL HOUSE

FIGURE 26

This house is suggested in part by a picture of the Nathan Hale Schoolhouse in Alice Morse Earle's *Child Life in Colonial Days*, but chiefly by the floor plan in Abbott's "Rodolphus," *Harpers Magazine*, Vol. 4., 1851, page 441.

FIGURE 27

This floorplan is taken from Abbott's "Rodolphus," *Harper's Magazine*, Vol. 4, 1851, page 444.

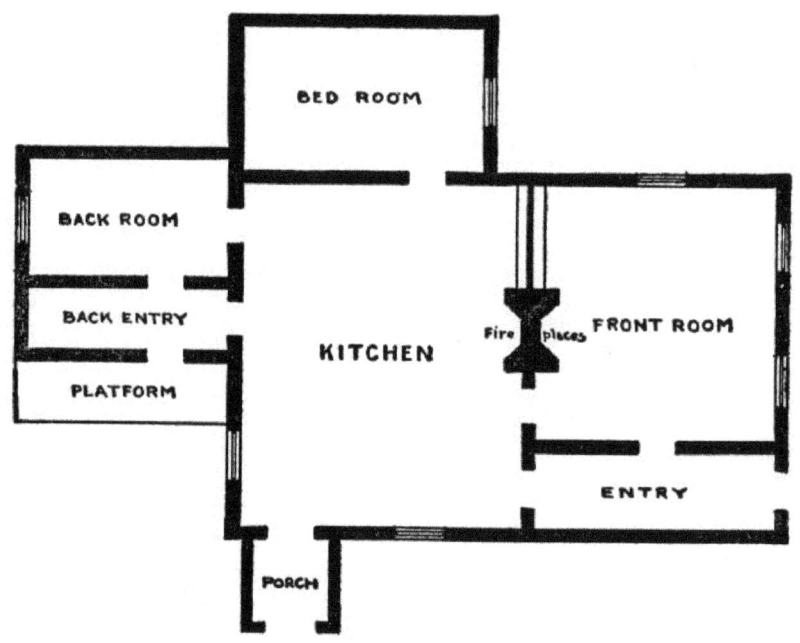

FIGURE 27. FLOOR PLAN

BED ROOM

BACK ROOM

BACK ENTRY

FRONT ROOM

Fire places

KITCHEN

PLATFORM

ENTRY

PORCH

PLATE I
COLONIAL KITCHEN IN THE NEWARK MUSEUM

The room in which the kitchen was built at the Newark Museum is about 31' × 75'. One carpenter, with very little assistance, constructed the kitchen in a few days. A house-painter painted it in about two days. Its total cost, ready for furniture, was not over one hundred and seventy-five dollars.

PLATE II
COLONIAL FIRESIDE

A picture of the fireplace at one end of an old time kitchen which was set up in the Newark Library, 1916. Notes on its construction are given on pp. 49-51.

PLATE III
DOMESTIC INDUSTRY

How the colonial kitchen was used as sewing room and nursery. The end of the kitchen through whose window is seen the landscape painted on screens and the barberry bush standing in a pot on the floor.

PLATE IV
TEA TIME

An old-time dining-table set with old-time china and pewter and lighted with candles. The end of the kitchen shows the corner cupboard, shelves for dishes and hooks for tippets and mittens.

Milton Keynes UK
Ingram Content Group UK Ltd.
UKHW051025250324
439991UK00008B/1025